INTERRUPTING CHICKEN

INTERRUPTING CHICKEN

David Ezra Stein

SCHOLASTIC INC.
New York Toronto London Auckland
Sydney Mexico City New Delhi Hong Kong

It was bedtime for the little red chicken.

"Okay, my little chicken," said Papa.
"Are you all ready to go to sleep?"

"Yes, Papa! But you forgot something."

"What's that?" asked Papa.

"A bedtime story!"

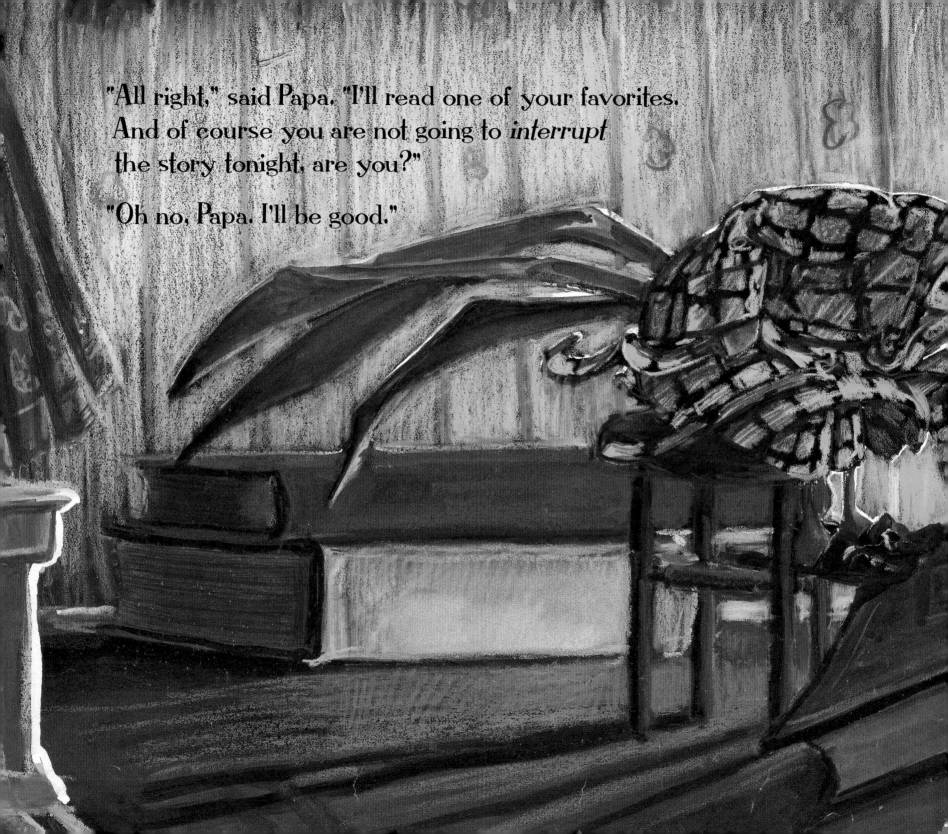

"All right," said Papa. "I'll read one of your favorites.
And of course you are not going to *interrupt*
the story tonight, are you?"

"Oh no, Papa. I'll be good."

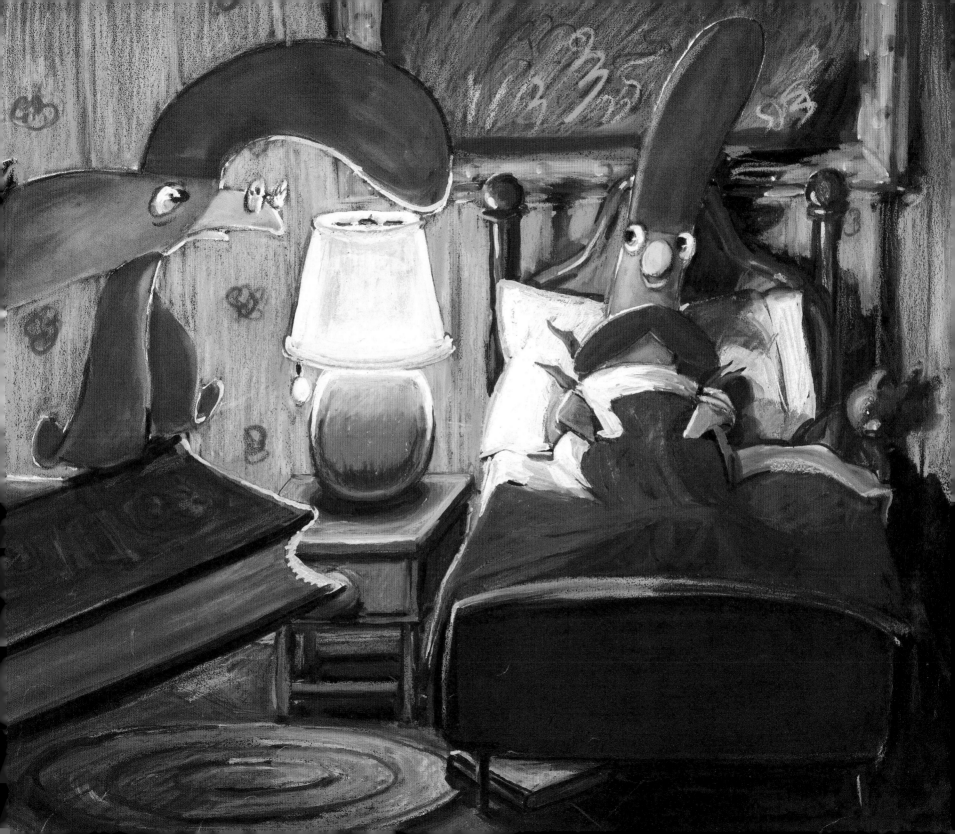

Hansel and Gretel were very hungry. Deep in the woods they found a house made of candy. Nibble, nibble, nibble; they began to eat the house, until the old woman who lived there came out and said, "What lovely children! Why don't you come inside?" They were just about to follow her when—

"Chicken."

"Yes, Papa?"

"You interrupted the story. Try not to get so involved."

"I'm sorry, Papa. But she really was a witch."

"Well, you're supposed to be relaxing so you can fall asleep."

"Let's try another story. I'll be good!"

"Take this basket of goodies to Grandma," said Little Red Riding Hood's mother. "But don't stray from the path. The woods are full of danger." Red Riding Hood skipped along through the deep woods. By and by she met a wolf who wished her "Good morning." She was about to answer him when—

"Chicken."

"Yes, Papa?"

"You did it again. You interrupted two stories,
and you're not even sleepy!"

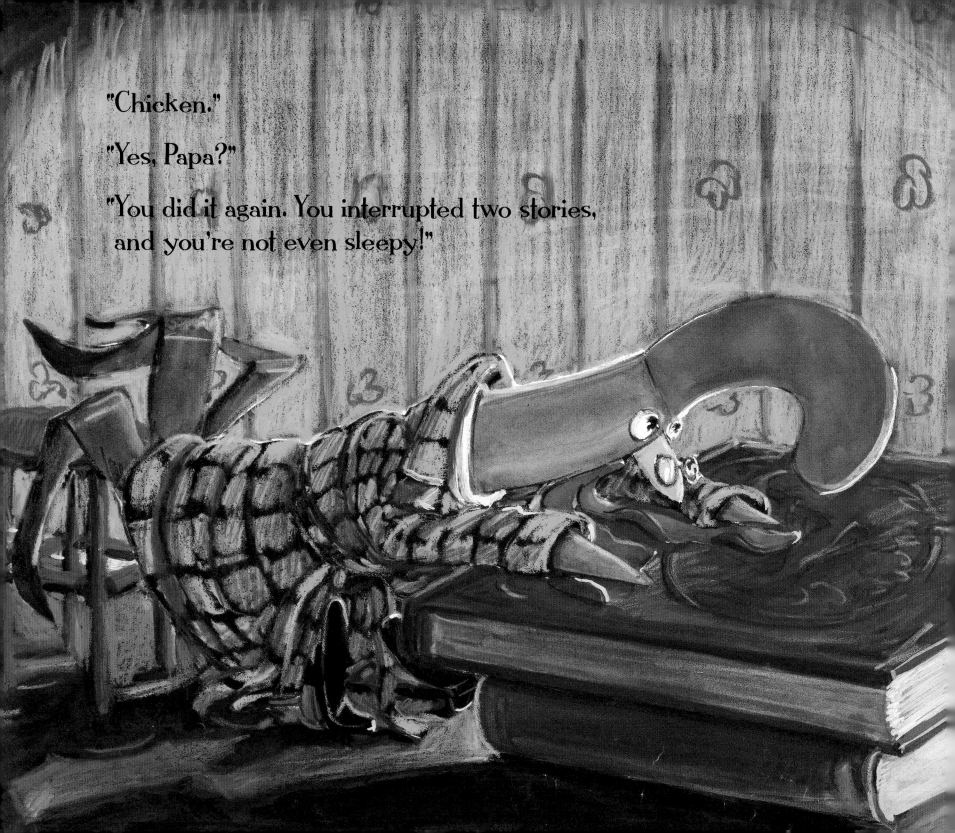

"I know, Papa! I'm sorry. But he was a *mean* old wolf."

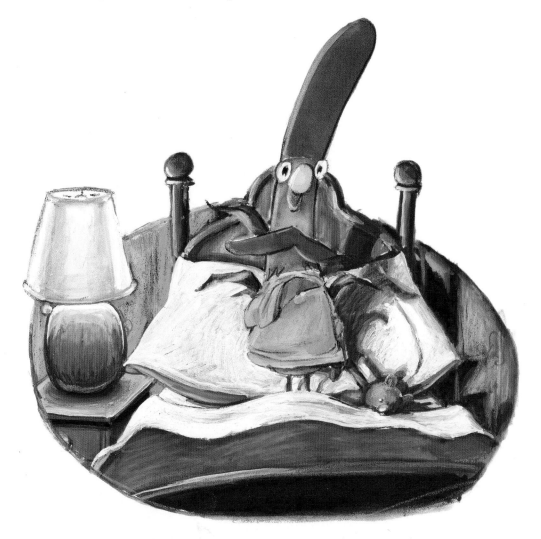

"Yes. Now get back into bed."

"Okay, Papa. Let's try one more *little* story, and I'll be good!"

Chicken Little was hit on the head by an acorn. *The sky is falling!* she thought.

She was about to run off and warn Goosey Loosey, Ducky Lucky, Henny Penny,

and everyone on the farm the sky was falling when—

"Chicken."

"Yes, Papa?"

"You did it AGAIN."

"Oh, Papa. I couldn't let that little chicken get all upset over an acorn! Please read *one more* story, and I promise I'll fall asleep."

"But Chicken," said Papa, "we are out of stories."

"Oh no, Papa. I can't go to sleep without a story!"

"Then," said Papa, yawning, "why don't *you* tell *me* a story?"

"*Me* tell a story?" said the little red chicken. "Okay, Papa! Here we go! Um . . ."

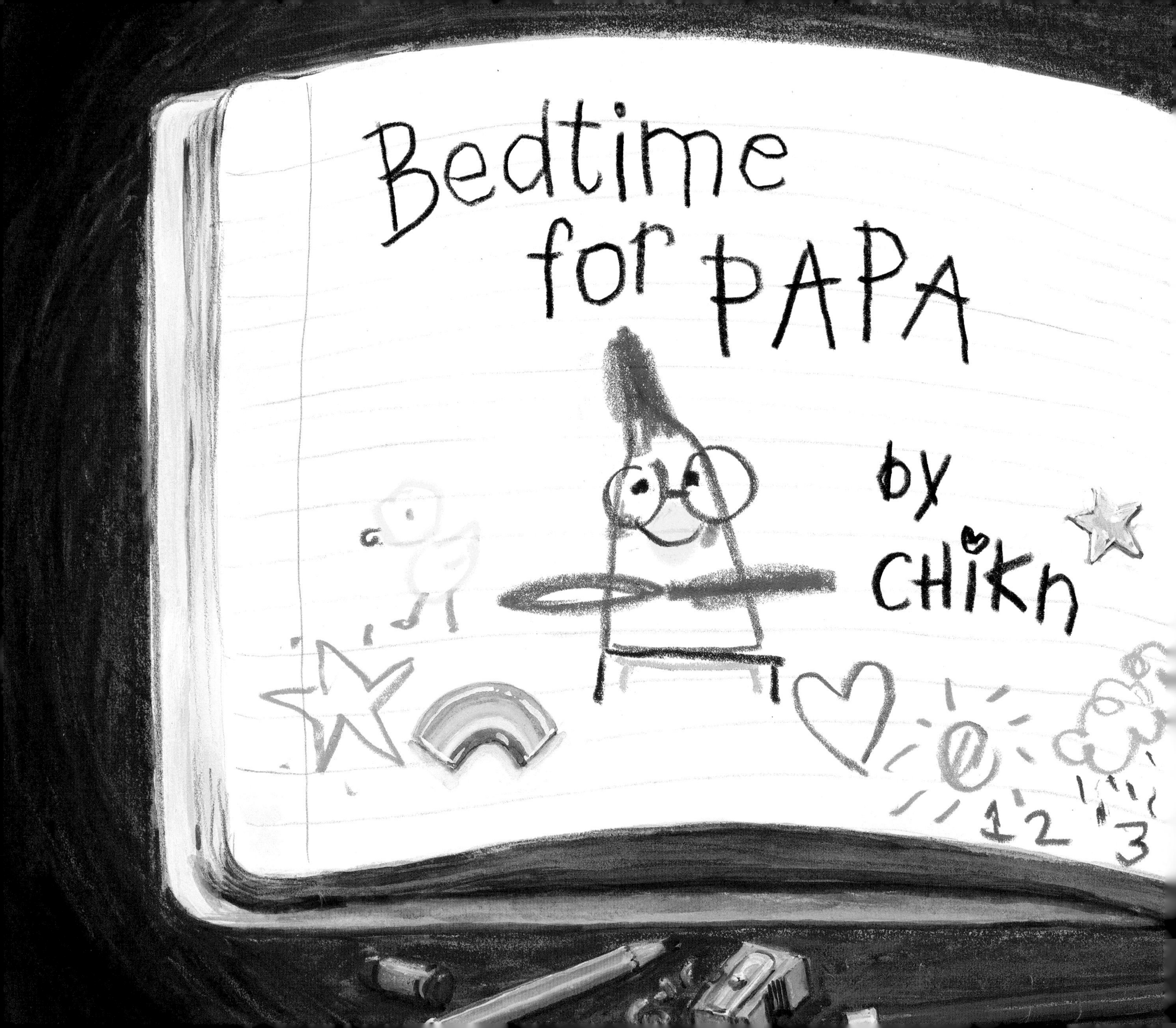
Bedtime for PAPA
by CHiKn
1 2 3

Once there was a little red chicken who put her Papa to bed. She read him a hundred stories. She even gave him warm milk, but nothing worked: he stayed wide awake all—

"Good night, Papa."

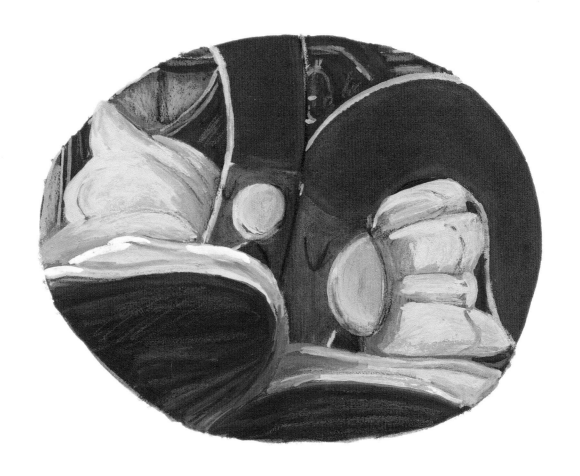

THE END

For Bibi

Many thanks to Rebecca, Sarah, and Ann for helping put this book to bed.

ISBN 978-0-545-39124-5

12 11 10 9 8 7 6 5 4 3 2 1   11 12 13 14 15 16/0

Printed in Singapore   46

First Scholastic printing, September 2011

This book was typeset in Malonia Voigo.
The illustrations were done in watercolor, water-soluble crayon,
china marker, pen, opaque white ink, and tea.